THE LITTLE CUPCAKES

by Anthony King

illustrated by

Sue Hellard

CUPCAKE PUBLISHING

Published by Cupcake Publishing
Designed by David Butler

Publisher's Cataloging-in-Publication

King, Anthony, 1937-
    The little cupcakes / by Anthony King; illustrated
by Sue Hellard.
    p. cm.
    SUMMARY: A young girl brings cupcakes to school
to share with her classmates, but a problem arises
because the cupcakes are not all decorated the same.
The child's father uses the event as an opportunity to
teach her about tolerance for differences.
    Audience: Ages 4-10.
    ISBN 0-9752786-1-4

1. Difference (Psychology)—Juvenile fiction.
2. Fathers and daughters—Juvenile fiction.
[1. Individuality—Fiction. 2. Fathers and daughters—
Fiction.]   I. Hellard, Susan, ill. II. Title.

PZ7.K5715Lit 2005   [E]
                      QBI05-600041

PRINTED IN CHINA

10 9 8 7 6 5 4 3 2

Cupcake Publishing
38 E. Ridgewood Ave.
Suite 132
Ridgewood, New Jersey 07450

For My Little Cupcakes

Caitlin McDermott King

Megan Barrett King

AK

Caitlin came running downstairs very happy and excited. It was her birthday and her Daddy was taking her to the bakery to pick up cupcakes for her friends at school.

Her eyes widened in delight at the sight of all the goodies, and her mouth watered from the delicious smells. She saw funny little smiley-face vanilla and chocolate cupcakes with eyes and mouths made of colorful sprinkles. There were only ten vanillas and two chocolates left, so she chose them all.

Dad dropped her off at school and she ran to her classroom eager to share the cupcakes with her friends.

"But they're not all the same," said Ms. Simmons.

"Can we choose?" asked Caitlin.

Later, when Caitlin came home from school, she carried a package. "How was your party, dear?" Dad asked.

"Okay," she said as she handed him the package with a look of sadness on her usually smiley face.

Inside, neatly lined up, were the tops of the little cupcakes, their sprinkled eyes and grins now lopsided after hours of rough handling.

Dad was shocked. "Wha...what happened?"

"Ms. Simmons took the tops off because they weren't all the same. She was afraid someone would get chocolate instead of vanilla and be unhappy."

"Did someone complain?" Dad asked.

"No. We liked them the way they were." A tear rolled down her cheek.

Caitlin sat down and Dad said,
"There is nothing in this world
that's exactly the same, dear."

"The world itself isn't the same.

It's egg-shaped and
funky at the poles."

"Trees aren't the same.

Some are big,

some are small."

"Grass isn't the same.

Some is yellow-green,

some is blue-green.

Snowflakes aren't alike.

Each is different."

"People aren't the same.

Some are tall,

some are short.

Some are thin, some are round."

"Some are white,

some are yellow,

and some are black.

Some are smart, and some aren't so smart."

"Feelings aren't all the same.

Some people care about animals,

and some care about

trips to the moon."

"Even level playing fields aren't exactly the same."

"If everything in the world was created differently, Daddy, why do some people want them to be the same?"

"Because they think the world would be better," he said, "but it wouldn't be."

"If everything in the world were the same, all growth would stop, all learning would stop, and all love would stop."

"We'd all look alike, think alike, feel alike, and act alike.

Would you like that?"

"No, Daddy, I want to be me," Caitlin replied.

"And I love you because you're you," Daddy smiled.

"We don't need things to be the same. We need to accept that people, places, and things are different and that differences are okay."

"That's tolerance."

"Ms. Simmons had a different idea from yours, but that's okay, too."

"Is there nothing in the whole, whole world that's the same, Daddy?" she asked.

"My love for you and your love for me is the same, my darling," he smiled.

Caitlin thought a moment and said, "No, Daddy, I love you more."

Daddy hugged her and didn't tell her she was wrong.

GUIDE FOR PARENTS AND TEACHERS

The Little Cupcakes provides an excellent opportunity for parents and teachers to engage children in an exploration of differences and diversity. In particular, the ways in which people are both similar and different.

When parents and teachers work together, they become powerful partners in the education of children. Whether in the classroom or at home, parents and teachers have a long-term impact a child's values and attitudes.

Here are a few discussion questions that will help illustrate the key points of this story.

- Read the story with your child/student and listen to how they respond to what happens to Caitlin.

Ask how they feel about what happened to Caitlin. Ask if anything like that has ever happened to them. How did they feel?

- Children love stories, and the most important thing a parent/teacher can do is read to them aloud. However, the more you involve the child in the process by allowing them to ask questions the deeper understanding they will achieve; make the reading process interactive.

Read the story again, and ask if Caitlin or her classmates would have had a problem if the tops were not taken off the cupcakes. What would have been a fair way to decide who got the two chocolate cupcakes?

- Teachers and parents can use books to help children understand situations that they will encounter with their families, friends and at school.

Ask if they think what Caitlin's dad said about nothing in the world being exactly the same is true. What are some examples of how differences in the world benefit us? What are some ways you are different from your friends, classmates or others in your family? What are some ways you are the same?

- When parents and teachers help their children to read, their children develop increased language and vocabulary skills, increased interest in books, greater enjoyment in reading, and increased self-esteem.

Talk with your child/student about individual words that may be used in a new way. Diversity – Tolerance – Differences – Disappointment – Acceptance – Same – Love. Ask them what these words mean to them now.

Children who learn with love, love to learn.